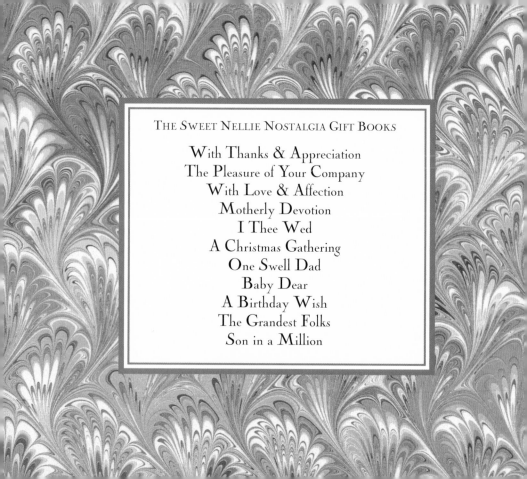

My Delightful Daughter

To ————————————————

From ————————————————

$\mathcal{B}$e honest and sincere, and willing to take bravely a part of the responsibility of the life you desire to enjoy. $\mathcal{G}$ood women are more valuable to a country than great men, and $\mathcal{A}$merican girls are the very stuff of which the best women can be made.

—Jennie June
Talks on Women's Topics
1864

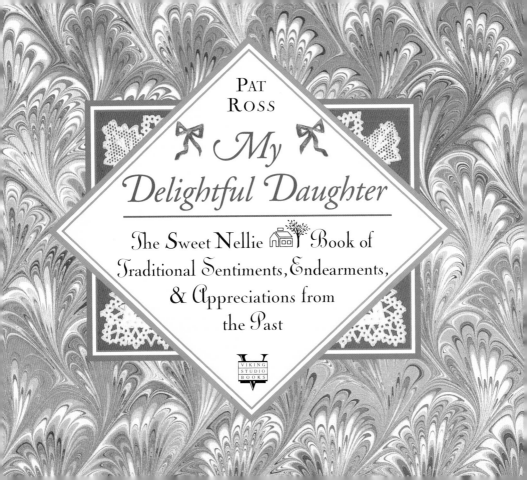

PAT ROSS

My Delightful Daughter

The Sweet Nellie Book of
Traditional Sentiments, Endearments,
& Appreciations from
the Past

VIKING
STUDIO
BOOKS

VIKING STUDIO BOOKS
Published by the Penguin Group
Penguin Books USA Inc., 375 Hudson Street, New York, New York 10014, U.S.A.
Penguin Books Ltd, 27 Wrights Lane, London W8 5TZ, England
Penguin Books Australia Ltd, Ringwood, Victoria, Australia
Penguin Books Canada Ltd, 10 Alcorn Avenue,
Toronto, Ontario, Canada M4V 3B2
Penguin Books (N.Z.) Ltd, 182-190 Wairau Road, Auckland 10, New Zealand

Penguin Books Ltd, Registered Offices: Harmondsworth, Middlesex, England

First published in 1994 by Viking Penguin,
a division of Penguin Books USA Inc.

1 3 5 7 9 10 8 6 4 2

ISBN 0-670-85010-1
CIP data available

Printed in Singapore   Set in Nicholas Cochin
Marbled endpaper design © 1992 by Mimi Schleicher
Designed by Virginia Norey *for Danika*
and by Amy Hill

INTRODUCTION

$\mathcal{T}$he meaning of the word *daughter* is such a personal and individual thing. Fathers are said to dote on daughters; mothers are said to value the child in their image. Together as parents we alternately praise their accomplishments and anguish over their escapades. Yet we treasure them from the moment someone says, "It's a girl!"

I learned of the gender of my child in a crowded New York subway during rush hour. It was November 1972, and I was clutching the center pole, since straphanging was too awkward a position for a woman almost nine months pregnant. There we were, packed in like sardines, all seeking space on the same pole, leaning shoulder to shoulder as the train lurched, avoiding eye contact in that typically New York way.

Those were the days before routine sonograms and gender tests. Back then, you prepared a list of girl names and one of boy names for the big day. I refused to acknowledge the gender of my heart's desire, though I did have my secret hope.

All of a sudden, on that crowded subway car, I grew aware of a beautiful dark-eyed woman staring at me. Her hand was the one next to mine on the metal pole. I smiled, and she nodded—bold acts during morning rush! For the next several stops, I had the oddest feeling that we were sharing a secret. I quickly dismissed my pregnant imagination. But when the train pulled into the station a stop before mine, the woman reached across the pole that divided us and gently touched my very obvious abdomen with the tips of her fingers. At that exact moment, she uttered something in Spanish that sounded like a hasty prayer or a blessing. Then, "Niña," she said to me. I translated silently: *A girl*. My heart's desire. Without another word, this stranger disappeared through the closing doors.

When our daughter was born, Joel and I took the girl name at the top of our list, the one we had decided on together: Erica. Then I got to choose her middle name: Hope. And I recalled the stranger on the subway who has lingered in my memory. *It was just a good guess*, I sometimes chide myself. Maybe.

Precious
Treasures

*O*ur daughters are the most precious of our treasures, the dearest possessions of our homes and the objects of our most watchful love.

—Margaret E. Sangster
Fairest Girlhood
1906

*B*e sure, then, that you are a good daughter. It is the best preparation for every other station, and will be its own reward.

—T. S. Arthur
Our Homes
1866

*M*any daughters have done virtuously, but thou excellest them all.

—Proverbs 31:29

*T*he younger your daughter, the more apt she is to love you.

—E. W. Howe
Country-Town Sayings
1911

*T*he sympathetic, winsome daughter and sister! Literature has recorded again and again her work of bringing sunshine and fragrant balm to sorely tried hearts in the household.

—Mary A. Laselle
The Young Woman Worker
1914

$\mathcal{A}$ daughter is an embarrassing and ticklish possession.

—Menander
Perinthis
c. 300 B.C.

*Her
Mother's
Image*

O mare pulchra filia pulchrior.
O fairer daughter of a fair mother.

—Horace
Odes (I, xvi, i)
65–8 B.C.

*T*he companion,
the friend, and
confidante of her
mother . . .

—Richard Steele
The Tattler
May 23, 1710

$\mathcal{T}$he mother should guide her daughter in all she does, and the daughter should abide her mother's decisions. Otherwise that sacred, beautiful friendship that can be created only between a mother and daughter will never exist.

—Lillian Eichler
Book of Etiquette
1922

A mother's example sketches the outline of her child's
character.

—Mrs. H. O. Ward
Sensible Etiquette
1878

*T*here can be no more delightful sight in a home than the daughter who is the respectful, deferential, loving comrade of her mother; the daughter who by pleasant, winning manners helps to keep the wheels of the machinery of the family well oiled, the members of the family happy; the daughter who lightens the cares of her mother and by her winsome, thoughtful presence, puts more cheer, more courage, and more real happiness into the life of the household; the daughter whose manner toward all the small events of each day is such as to make the lovely flower of contentment blossom in the home.

—Mary A. Laselle
The Young Woman Worker
1914

Daughter am I in my mother's house,
But mistress in my own.

—Rudyard Kipling
Our Lady of the Snows
1897

$\mathcal{T}$he feeling that enables anyone to be unkind to a mother will make her who indulges it wretched for life.

—T. S. Arthur
Our Homes
1866

The
Fortunate
Father

*T*here is a very delicate bond of sympathy and friendship between the father and his daughter.

—Margaret E. Sangster
The Art of Home Making
1898

I am all the daughters of my father's house
And all the brothers too.

—William Shakespeare
Twelfth Night (II, iv, 123)
1599

*T*he lucky man has a daughter as his first child.

—Spanish proverb

$\mathcal{A}$nd he shall turn
the heart of the fathers
to the children
and the heart of the children
to the fathers.

—Malachi 4:6

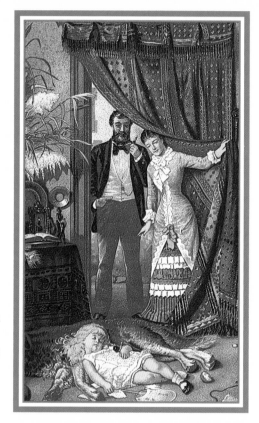

*H*is daughter will say, "Papa, do look here just one minute!
How do you like my new gown?" And the answer never varies:
"Very pretty, indeed. I hope it's paid for." —Lilian Bell
From a Girl's Point of View
1897

*M*argaret: Dad, if I should ever marry—not that I will, but if I should—at the marriage ceremony will you let me be the one who says "I do"?

—J. M. Barrie
Dear Brutus
1917

$\mathcal{W}$*ho giveth this woman to this man?* The father, advancing between the bride and groom, takes his daughter's right hand, lays it in that of the groom, bowing his acquiescence as he murmurs, *I do*.

—Emily Holt
Encyclopedia of Etiquette
1921

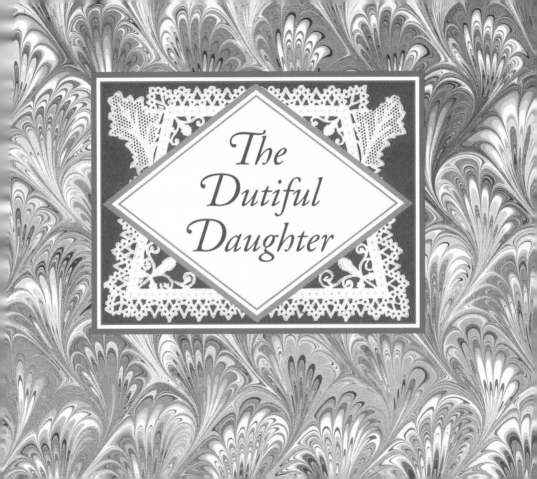

The
Dutiful
Daughter

*T*he young girl should follow her mother's example and advice in all things.

—Lillian Eichler
Book of Etiquette
1922

*T*he girl who is properly nourished and who engages in a needful amount of muscular activity (so much as possible in the open air) is quite certain to grow up into healthy physical womanhood, especially if she be intelligent and reasonable in the matters of dress and mental occupation.

—Lyman B. Sperry, M.D.
Confidential Talks with Young Women
1898

*P*arents, especially mothers, should also watch with a jealous care the tendencies of their daughters' affections; and if they see them turning toward unworthy or undesirable objects, influence of some sort should be brought to bear to counteract this.

—John H. Young
Our Deportment
1882

$\mathcal{N}$o mother has any right to allow her young daughters to ruin their tempers, health, and complexions, by lying in bed till nine or ten o'clock. Early rising conduces more to the preservation of health, freshness, and young looks, than anything in the world, and even to the proper preservation of our mental faculties.

—*Good Manners; A Manual of Etiquette in Good Society*
1870

*O*nce women taught their daughters house-keeping and sewing from stern principle, and made it neither beautiful nor attractive. Then house-keeping went out of fashion.

—Lilian Bell
From a Girl's Point of View
1897

*T*he daughter of a busy mother makes a bad housekeeper.

—Irish proverb

$\mathcal{T}$he wise mother, training her daughter not for the moment but for all time, will realize that there are no small things where a child is concerned; that some things, apparently the most trivial, will have far-reaching results, and therefore with a critical eye she will scan all influences that surround the infant and eliminate all that seem in the least calculated to interfere with her most harmonious development.

—Mary Wood-Allen
A Mother's Year
1905

The daughters of a house, when a ball is given, may dress with great elegance, but should be careful to make no effort to outshine their guests.

—Emily Holt
Encyclopedia of Etiquette
1921

*I*n olden days notable housekeepers were notable women. In managing their homes and servants, training their daughters in homely fashion to bake and stew, spin and embroider, or concoct the herbal remedies needed for the relief of their poorer neighbours as well as themselves, the worthy dames seem to have found sufficient distinction as well as employment.

—Mrs. Isabella Beeton
Every-Day Cookery and Housekeeping Book
c. 1860

The American Girl

*L*ife is no longer shown to the young daughter as a plaything by fond parents who plan no future except marriage and social success for the young woman whose future rests in their hands. To-day life is shown to her as it is shown to her brother—as something beautiful, something impressive, something worthy of deep thought and ambitious plans.

—Lillian Eichler
Book of Etiquette
1922

*I*f you let your daughters grow up idle, perhaps under the mistaken impression that as you yourselves have had to work hard they shall know only enjoyment, you are preparing them to be useless to others and burdens to themselves.

—Theodore Roosevelt

*P*arents should always be perfectly familiar with the character of their daughter's associates, and they should exercise their authority so far as not to permit her to form any improper acquaintances. In regulating the social relations of their daughter, parents should bear in mind the possibility of her falling in love with anyone with whom she may come in frequent contact. Therefore, if any gentleman of her acquaintance is particularly ineligible as a husband, he should be excluded as far as practicable from her society.

—John H. Young
Our Deportment
1882

$\mathcal{M}$ake the family life a model of courtesy and good manners, and the sons and daughters, when they go out into the world, will be in no danger of attracting the ill-bred and vicious.

—A. E. Davis
American Etiquette and Rules of Politeness
1882

*P*arents should carefully watch the young gentlemen who frequent their houses, *i.e.*, should see that undesirable intimacies are not formed with their daughters, for friendships and intimacies soon lead to love.

—N.C.
Practical Etiquette
1881

*P*arents must be what they wish their children to be, and when once this great truth has taken possession of a mother's mind, her child becomes her educator, leading her forward, and developing her as no other influence can lead her.

—Mrs. H. O. Ward
Sensible Etiquette
1878

*I*t seems fitting that a book about traditions of the past should be decorated with period artwork. In that spirit, the art in *My Delightful Daughter* has been taken from personal collections of original nineteenth- and early-twentieth-century drawings, advertising cards, photographs, and other paper treasures of the time.

The endpapers and chapter openings contain a pattern reproduced from a favorite marbelized paper.